ANIMALS EVERYWHERE

Books by Ingri and Edgar Parin d'Aulaire

ABRAHAM LINCOLN

ANIMALS EVERYWHERE

BENJAMIN FRANKLIN

BUFFALO BILL

DON'T COUNT YOUR CHICKS

FOXIE

GEORGE WASHINGTON

LEIF THE LUCKY

THE LORD'S PRAYER

NILS

OLA

OLA AND BLAKKEN

POCAHONTAS

THE STAR SPANGLED BANNER

TOO BIG

WINGS FOR PER

ANIMALS EVERYWHERE

by Ingri and Edgar Parin d'Aulaire

DOUBLEDAY & COMPANY, INC., GARDEN CITY, NEW YORK

Copyright 1940, 1954 by Doubleday & Company, Inc.
Library of Congress Catalog Card Number 54-5904
All Rights Reserved. Lithographed in the U. S. A.

ANIMALS EVERYWHERE

Far to the South, where it is very hot, live the animals that like very hot weather. There the lively Monkey hides in the leaves. The shy Zebra gallops over the grass. The fat Hippopotamus rises yawning out of the river. The haughty Giraffe peers over the tallest trees. The Ostrich fluffs its fine tail feathers.

The swift little Antelope runs to save its life. The Chimpanzee chatters in the treetops. The Anteater uses its long nose to dig up anthills. The wise Elephant is so strong he can uproot trees with his trunk. The little Mouse darts hither and thither.

The Mouse squeaks. The Monkey chatters. The Antelope cries.

The Anteater sniffles. The Elephant trumpets.

The Giraffe is mute. The Zebra squeals.

The Ostrich booms. The Hippopotamus bellows.

The ferocious Tiger jumps to attack its prey. The dangerous Lion is the king of the beasts. The Ape walks on two or on four and is much like a man. The Rhinoceros defends himself with the horn on his nose.

The Dromedary with one hump, the Camel with two, can walk for weeks without drinking. The Crocodile lies still like a log. Where these animals live it is never cold and never winter. Sometimes the rain comes down in torrents, but most of the time the burning sun scorches.

The Camel and the Dromedary groan. The Parrot talks.

The Crocodile smacks its jaw.

The Rhinoceros snorts.   The Tiger snarls.

The Ape screeches.   The Lion roars.

The animals that like weather neither too hot nor too cold live where we live. Here the shaggy Buffalo roams. The Deer plays. The sly Fox sneaks. The Skunk defends himself with his smell.

The noble Horse trots. The proud Cock stalks. The busy Hen scratches. The lively Squirrel gathers nuts. The Donkey balks. The Cat prowls.

The Donkey brays.   The Horse whinnies.   The Squirrel scolds.

The Cat miaows.   The Cock crows.

The Fox yaps. The Skunk rattles.

The Deer bugles. The Buffalo lows.

The Goose waddles. The friendly Cow chews its cud. The mischievous Billy Goat bucks. The Eagle soars through the air. The peaceful Sheep grazes. The Duck walks on the ground, swims in the water, and flies through the air. The Dog hunts.

The sleepy Bear hibernates in winter. The busy Beaver builds dams. The Moose lives in the deep forests. Where these animals live it is cold in winter and warm in summer.

The Moose coughs. The Bear grumbles.

The Beaver splashes. The Eagle screams.

The Dog barks.　　　The Sheep baas.　　　The Cow moos.

The Duck quacks.　　The Goat bleats.　　The Goose honks.

Far to the North live the animals that like cold weather. The Reindeer digs for grass and moss under the snow. The cruel Wolf pursues his prey. The timid Hare tries to hide. The black Raven steals (like a raven).

The Owl is very wise. The horned Narwhale swims through the icy waters. The sleek Seal crawls up on ice floes to rest. The Eider Duck gives us eiderdowns.

The Eider Duck squawks. The Owl hoots.

The Seal barks. The Narwhale swishes.

The Raven croaks.   The Wolf howls.

The Reindeer pants.   The Hare thumps.

The Walrus has a very thick hide. The Sea Lion is heavy and clumsy. The Whale spurts water out of a hole in his head.

The Sea Gull sails through the air and dives into the sea for fish. The Polar Bear is a ferocious beast. Where these animals live there is snow and ice all through the year. In summer the sun never goes down and in winter it never rises.

The Polar Bear growls.   The Gull cries.

The Whale blows, and he is the biggest

The Sea Elephant roars.

of all the animals on land and in the sea.

The Walrus snores.